If Peace is...

If Peace is...

by Jane Baskwill

Illustrated by Stephanie Carter

If peace is a candle,
I'll light one each night.

If peace is a hand,
I'll hold on so tight.

If peace is a bell,
I'll make it ring.

If peace is a song,
I'll want to sing.

If peace is a gift,
I'll open it with care.

If peace is a treasure,
I'll search everywhere.

If peace is a garden,
I'll tend every seed.

If peace is a book,
I'll have to read.

But peace is more than all of these things,
more than a book or a bell that rings.

It's more than the work of just one or two.

Peace is the work that we all must do.

Peace is a promise
we make one another . . .

. . . to love and protect,

and to care for each other.

It’s a hand waved in friendship,
a smile on a face . . .

...a kind word and deed,
any time, any place.

Peace is a promise—
it's something we do.

For peace is a promise
kept always by you!

To the staff and students of Kingston and District School who inspired this poem : May peace be in your life as well as in your mind and heart.
—J.B.

To Fraser
—S.C.

For information contact:
MONDO Publishing
980 Avenue of the Americas
New York, NY 10018
Visit our website at www.mondopub.com

Printed in China
07 08 09 10 11 12 HC 9 8 7 6 5 4 3
07 08 09 10 11 12 PB 9 8 7 6 5 4

ISBN 1-59034-448-0 (hardcover) ISBN 1-59034-449-9 (pbk.)

Designed by Edward Miller

Library of Congress Cataloging-in-Publication Data

Baskwill, Jane.
If peace is a promise / by Jane Baskwill ; illustrated by Stephanie Carter.
p. cm.
Summary: Illustrations and rhyming text describe what peace is.
ISBN 1-59034-448-0 (hc.) – ISBN 1-59034-449-9 (pbk.)
[1. Peace--Fiction. 2. Stories in rhyme.] I. Carter, Stephanie, 1965- ill. II. Title.

PZ8.3.B2896 If 2003 [E]--dc21

2002029351